Wait for Me!

Written by Jane E. Gerver
Illustrated by Mick Reid

children's press®

A Division of Scholastic Inc.
New York Toronto London Auckland Sydney
Mexico City New Delhi Hong Kong
Danbury, Connecticut

Library of Congress Cataloging-in-Publication Data

Gerver, Jane E.
  Wait for me! / written by Jane E. Gerver ; illustrated by Mick Reid.
      p. cm. — (My first reader)
  Summary: No one will wait for a little boy who is always late until he finds a friend who is late too.
  ISBN 0-516-24676-3 (lib. bdg.)   0-516-25116-3 (pbk.)
  [1. Punctuality—Fiction. 2. Stories in rhyme.] I. Reid, Mick, ill. II. Title. III. Series.
  PZ8.3+
  [E]—dc22
                                    2004000237

Published in 2004 by Children's Press, an imprint of Scholastic Library Publishing.
Published simultaneously in Canada.
Printed in the United States of America.

CHILDREN'S PRESS and associated logos are trademarks and or
registered trademarks of Scholastic Library Publishing. SCHOLASTIC and
associated logos are trademarks and or registered trademarks of Scholastic Inc.

1 2 3 4 5 6 7 8 9 10 R 13 12 11 10 09 08 07 06 05 04

Note to Parents and Teachers

Once a reader can recognize and identify the 37 words used to tell this story, he or she will be able to successfully read the entire book. These 37 words are repeated throughout the story, so that young readers will be able to recognize the words easily and understand their meaning.

The 37 words used in this book are:

am	for	my	that
and	get	not	the
anybody	gone	now	too
are	I	please	wait
bus	I'll	run	what
clock	is	says	will
do	last	should	you
done	late	slow	
dressed	me	stop	
fast	must	teacher	

My clock is slow!

I get dressed fast.

7

The bus is gone.

Now I am last.

Please wait for me!

I am not done!

My teacher says I must not run.

our class

Is that clock fast?

Now I am late!

Will anybody stop and wait?

23

Please wait for me!

What should I do?

Are you late, too?

I'll wait for you!

ABOUT THE AUTHOR

Jane E. Gerver is the author of many children's books, ranging from preschool board books to middle-grade fiction. She lives with her husband and daughter in New York City, where she is always rushing to get to places on time!

ABOUT THE ILLUSTRATOR

Mick Reid spent the 1970s playing the guitar in rock bands. In the 1980s, he switched from music to art and in 1989, graduated with honors from the Liverpool School of Art. Since then, Reid has illustrated more than 250 books. He and his wife, Eugénie, live in Wirral, England, with their cat, Nellie.